Best Wedding Ever

Book*Squirrel* Publication

Book*Squirrel* Publication

Regd. Under MSME Act.

"Best Wedding Ever"

By: Avani Singhal

ISBN: 978-93-89557-07-7

English Fictional

1st Edition

Cover: Mr_Ash

Price: INR199

Acknowledgment

I would like to thank my family for supporting me and giving me the right to choose for myself, your approval is my biggest support.

A big THANK YOU to my editor-in-chief, AYUSH SHARMA for helping me, your contribution made all the difference.

Thank you so much Raunak Rishabh for motivating me to follow my passion, for believing in me. And a very big thanks to Pushpendra Tiwari, Prakhar Charan and my whole "chosen family" for their support and love throughout the journey.

Last but not the least thanks to Ashutosh Das for showing so much patience and helping me always.

Author's Bio

My name is Avani Singhal. I was born on 7th July 1999 in Kota (Rajasthan). I believe in a big life rather than a long one. Writing is my way to express my life in words as well as it's an escape for me from the real world. It keeps my mind at ease.

"Paper is my field, words are my army and pen is my sword,

I am a warrior defeating my own."

Instagram username : avi_7799

Index

End

PROLOGUE

And finally, the day arrives. The day I was waiting for, the day for which we have been preparing for the last few months, the day which has been our dream. The day when finally, "I and you will become us".

Everyone is here in Jodhpur for our grand destination wedding. My family, his family, all the relatives, and friends and of course our sweet little but not so little 18 kids.

All my 8 sweet little girls are helping me to get ready for this big day and so here I am sitting in front of the mirror savoring my last few minutes of being a bachelor. I am on the seventh cloud and looking at myself thinking about all the good and bad times that we suffered to finally reach this day.

Yipeeeee...........finally the day has arrived and I can't believe it, but I am the bride. My all little girls are looking beautiful and now they are happily welcoming their dear pops who is on the 'ghodi'. And of course, as per rituals I am not allowed to see the 'baraat'. But I know how happy everyone is and how madly my 10 little boys are dancing in the 'baraat' after all we have the technology, at least I can see my 'bachaas' if not my husband to be.

Chapter 1: First Day of College

On the First day of college, I was a bit nervous but as usual full of confidence being "I, me and myself". The orientation program was going on, and we were on our campus tour. All the students of different branches were aligned in single lines to walk through college and seniors were guiding us. College was government, not well maintained but still, it has its beauty as greenery was all around. I love nature much more than Salman khan loves his bracelet, so, I liked the environment and had made up my mind to spend my time in gardens more than from classrooms.

Seniors were giving us instruction on "how to behave" as we were the newbies in this college, so we have to go as per their demands.

I am a simple girl with a literally cute face. I know I am adoring myself but it's purely to describe myself. Seeing me for the first time you will think that I am the most innocent girl in town but to be true I am not. I was suffering from slight fever that day but still, I checked out all the boys, girls and seniors around. Everyone was busy in their own world, checking the college premises and in making new friends while I was busy checking everyone else.

And then, the moment arrived that I never thought of. I never knew that after this moment my life was going to change in a hasty manner. My vehicle of life is going to speed a 180-degree rotation.

A chill ran down my spine as soon as I saw him, my eyes got stuck to him. His back was at my side. I didn't move my eyes from him until he turned around. I became a statue, not realizing that I was staring at him. I checked his head to toe and was really engrossed with his attire. That feeling of sudden connection was weird, but I did not realize that my feelings were growing for someone, whom I just saw.

At first, he seemed handsome but not so handsome to me but, he was definitely attractive. Tall, dark and handsome, the deadliest combination of looks was in front of me. His body was well-toned, and he has this perfect body shape in his complete formals. I don't know why I felt this sudden connection with him, but I was completely attracted by his personality.

That day went well with this kind of feeling of attraction as well as the excitement of college life. I made a few girlfriends too from the same branch.

Soon, classes got started and strangers start becoming friends and more. New dreams, new plans were knitting roaming around this old college campus. #collegediaries is the people's new captions on Instagram tagging along with all the new friends of their own batch as well as others and seniors too.

College life is a new phase of life which is definitely a perfect combination of salt and sugar.

The life that everyone was waiting for along with the expectations that this phase we will enjoy to the hell and will taste each piece of it.

Similarly, I was dreaming of a life that I wanted to live on my rules so being a rebel I checked each and every part of college. Roamed in corridors like I am a senior. Even checked out the canteen in spite of senior's instructions "1st years are not allowed at the canteen." Attended each and every club's meetings, and registered myself for clubs that I found interesting.

CHAPTER 2: Friends or More?

After two weeks or so, one day when I was in a meet of a club, I spotted him there. I already decided somewhere inside my heart that I am always going to be present in this club meets and never go on leave so that I can get a chance anyhow to talk to him.

Somehow, I managed to know his name and other basic information. He was also in the Whatsapp group of the club, so I got his number damn easily but never approached, just checked his DP's as a single-sided lover.

For the first month, there was nothing we just cross paths in clubs' meetings but never talked. Maybe luck was on my side so destiny got us together. Main Freshers 2017 (of all branches together) was going to be held, luckily, I was the finalist and he was in the organizing committee, so we finally got on talking terms. I was the happiest person on earth that day. A feeling that can't be express in words.

"तुझे कुछ यूँ चाहा नजारो ने की काजल बना के खुद मै बसा लिया

और यूँ चाहा रूह ने की खुद को तुझमें बसा दिया ।"

He was busy giving instructions to people working on the stage when I blocked his way gathering all my courage and tried to talk starting from the question with a cute face and sweet voice, "boss, what I have to say in the introduction?"

Starting from this very question we talked for an hour, people do disturb us in between but still, we discussed every basic detail of the freshers and this is how our story started.

After the chat I happily went to the ladies' room to get ready for the event, I was too happy that everyone noticed me smiling sheepishly but I didn't care because what matters to me was him and my day was going way too good beyond words.

CHAPTER 3: FRESHERS; Best Day for Me

Freshers went well, it was organized in our college garden where all the main events are organized. The stage was decorated beautifully with colorful balloons, ribbons and of course the poster of freshers 2k17.

First-round was ramp walk which went well. The second round was a talent round and I gave my best in it too. One participant does a rap for more than a given time but still, he doesn't get disqualified and here starts the scam but teachers handled it. The last round was a question/answer round. My question was about politics. I hate politics and I don't even know 'p' of politics till now, I neither want to know. So, I messed up this round but it was ok for me though. I am never like the one who participates just to win, I am the one who participates only to enjoy and learn from participation.

I didn't get the title obviously but still, that day was the best day of my life. After the official party got over and teachers left, I just catch up with him for a while and thanked him for his guidance. As I turned to leave, at that moment he suddenly asked me to join him for the after-party. First, I got a little panicked as I was not expecting this as much early. This was too soon for me, yet I was too happy that this was happening. I go dumb but then controlling my senses and trying not to smile like an idiot, I happily said "yes" because obviously, I was more than happy and willing to spend time with him.

That was the night that we shared the dance floor as well as our friends. We danced on Rajasthani and Punjabi songs like idiots and enjoyed a lot. We even forgot that we were hungry and had not eaten anything for the whole evening. He became friends with my friends and I became friends with his friends. Also, we confirmed our "being single" relationship status so that we are sure that we can continue seeing each other.

And oh, I forgot to tell you one thing, being in a government college we don't get the privilege to do things per our wishes, we have to listen to our seniors and be a good junior if we don't want to be the ones dancing on bhajans on fresher's night. We can't call any of the senior anything other than "boss". So, I call him the boss instead of his name.

As all his friends get to know me on fresher's night, and they all were seniors and I was dancing and talking to them frequently being a junior, maybe I didn't get the title but I was the queen bee of the night, got famous pretty quickly in the college.

Chapter 4: The Perfect Relationship

After the night, Prithvi and I got spotted frequently in college corridors or gardens or in the library together by all our friends. We started chatting at night as well. Soon we became more than friends and the whole college got to know about this relationship of a senior and a junior. We too made it official, when he proposed me on chat and I said yes. I liked him a lot from the very first day of college. There was no chance that I will say no. Maybe he got a hint from my behavior since freshers' night, so he didn't take too much time in proposing me.

We were endgame. We were a perfect couple of that era, we have this perfect understanding of each other like Selina Gomez and Justin Bieber. Fascinating, I know.

Me being stubborn and free-spirited never wanted anyone to get into my personal space. My parents and grandmother have raised me to be a strong child who can handle things on her own, and I am not weird in a way to corrupt that legacy. He too understands my side, so, never interfered in my life neither did I at least at this starting phase of our love life. Whatever the thing is we decided that we will tell each other if we feel right, and we will never lie to each other. We can just simply hide things by saying that I am not feeling right to tell you about this right now, but we will not lie and once we said this we are not allowed to emotional blackmail each other to tell things, we will simply let things go.

He's being so mature, responsible and a bit introvert, he always says yes to my rules and everything I say. He was this perfect that his life just revolves around his friends, family and me. But he has the courage enough to expect me as his girlfriend around the college and this was the thing, I liked the most about him. I am always the fearless one, also I always dream of a person like this who will be proud to have me.

I liked him a lot and he liked me too. I always act crazy around him; I was the immature one in us. My love was growing, he was already mine but still, I have this feeling of love for him that I stare him in club meetings like I did before when we were not together. Everything was going well; we were enjoying being together. Meeting daily after lectures and chatting during boring lectures became our daily routine. For me, this was my first perfect relationship, and he was also doing his best on his part.

One day like Indian romantic movies he arranged a perfect date for us, I got really mesmerized by his act. At first, I know nothing about it. I don't know how many days did he was preparing for it. I was the only one who didn't know about this first date. Everyone else including his friends and mine knew about this including the fact that they were the ones who helped him to select the present as well as help him plan this beautiful date.

After our classes get over, he messaged me to meet him at the college gate, as soon as I got there, he was already there on a bike waiting for me and told me to hop on. I just did the same, as soon as we started riding, I started firing my questions about everything; who's that bike was, where are we going, why suddenly we are going out of college and at after 5 as I have to be at home at the time.

I was a localite and he was a hostelite; I have to be at home till 6, however, he has no restrictions.

We went for a long drive which was the very first experience for me. I always have seen this kind of romantic long drive on TV but never went to one. Being with him on the bike gives a very different feeling. We were on an empty road of Delhi city, so we have the advantage that we can't be seen that gave me a bit of relief. While Holding him tightly from behind I was not thinking of being seen or anything, I was just enjoying my first ride with him with all my feeling of love for him.

Winds were cold and the sun was on its verge to get disappeared in clouds of rising nightfall. Our bodies were heated and hearts were pounding fast. We go with the flow, enjoyed every bit of our drive but have to come back as I have to lead back home. We don't want to let this time go but time didn't stop for anyone, either we want it or not.

When we reached college, he presented me with a beautiful and shining bracelet for no reason, shared his feelings for the first time and thanked me for being his partner. He truly won my heart that day. He didn't say much but whatever he said his eyes proved. We completed each other. I too tried to confess my love but can't say much as I was full of feelings but was on lack of words, I thought expressing these feelings in words can be an insult to the feelings that we can show through posters and eyes, so we decided to leave words and just feel the feelings.

I truly loved the bracelet much more than I love my Choco pies.

"कुछ कहना है तुमसे

हां, मुझे कुछ कहना हे तुमसे

सिर्फ तुमसे

कुछ नजरो से बातें करनी है

कुछ लफ्ज़ो से बातें चुरानी है

इशारो की भाषा मे

अदाओं की वेशभूसा में

एक नयी ज़िन्दगी सजानी है

कुछ कहना है तुमसे

समां में गुम होकर

तुझ में चूर होकर

मुझे तिनको से घर बनाना है

पगडंडियों से सजाना है

कुछ ख्वाबो को हक़ीक़त बनाना है

कुछ तो कहना है तुमसे

पर अल्फ़ाज़ जुबान पर अटके है

मूड ऑफ है पर मुस्कुराने का मन है

लग रहा है ज़िन्दगी की आखिरी हवा महसूस कर रही हु

तुझे बाँहों में लेकर इतनी मेहफ़ूज़ सी लग रही हूँ

घास पर बैठे टिमटिमाते टारे भी कहने लगे है

की जैसे तुझे पाके

इस खूबसूरती मे

मैं और खूबसूरत लगने लगी हूँ

कुछ कहना है तुमसे

तुझ बिन अधूरी हूँ

हर रूप मैं तेरी हूँ

मेरे इस ख्वाबो के आसमान मे

मै तेरी कस्तूरी हूँ

इच्छुक हूँ

तुझमे मिलना चाहती हूँ

तेरा दिल इसलिए टटोला करती हूँ

की बहुत कुछ कहना चाहती हूँ

बहुत कुछ कहना चाहती हूँ । "

Chapter 5: First Kiss

Two months of time flawed just like seconds. We went on dates, one-day trips with friends and were happy to be together. Our relationship grew stronger day by day and we became pretty inseparable.

We were sitting at the back of the building of our college after the lectures. There were back doors that were now locked as college time is up and there was no one around. This was our regular meet up spot. We were spending a nice time, talking and laughing.

The climate was nice and beautiful, cold breeze were touching our bodies and was giving peace to our souls. Sun was about to set living the atmosphere golden around us like it was a roasted crispy cookie. Greenery can be seen everywhere but there were no signs of any living being anywhere expecting us.

The weather gives us the perfect romance feel and we flow with the feeling. Our eyes met, and we forget ourselves in that deep ocean of love, was on heights above skies. We got closer and closer and closer, so close that even the air can't pass from between us and our lips melt in each other's mouth for the very first time. He kissed me with all his feelings in his eyes and I kissed back carrying all the love inside me. We tasted the accent of each other with all the true feelings inside. It was like two flavors of ice cream melt inside each other.

We kissed passionately for more than 10 minutes only leaving each other in between gasping for air. We were not in the mood to let go of each other until my phone disturbed us. It was my mom and time was already 6:15 I broke the "get back home code" by 15 minutes and now was in trouble thinking what I am going to say where I was. So I disconnected the call and asked him what I am going to do now, he simply gave this idea to give the excuse of being in a club meeting and I applied the same. He already assured me that he will talk to the club members to support me in this if by chance my parents want to ask anyone. I was relieved but I had to reach home soon so I ran home quickly bidding him goodbye.

After reaching I just simply made the excuse, he told me and to my relief, my mother believed maybe because I was always the perfect daughter and broke the code first time in life and so finally, I took a breath of relief. I felt bad for lying to my mother but couldn't do anything about it so I just said sorry to her and god from deep down my heart.

 At night thinking about our first kiss and imagining our life for future I blushed sheep shy to myself and slept with all the dreams in my eyes not thinking about the possibilities or obstacles or negative side that may be on its way coming towards me from all sides cause life can neither as happy and peaceful as you thought, life can be unimaginably different.

"गुस्ताख़ है ये लब जो तुम्हारे लबो को छूने से डरते नहीं

याद करके वो पल मुझे तड़पाने से जरा भी मुकरते नहीं

मेरा वक़्त वक़्त से थोड़ा धीरे चल रहा है

तो कभी मेरा वक़्त वक़्त से आगे बढ़ रहा है

आने वाले कल का न मुझे पता न तुझे खबर

बस आज के सिद्दत भरे एहसासो में

मै खुदको तुझमे छोड़ आती हूँ । "

Chapter 6: Mechanical's Fresher's 2k17

The mechanical department is said to be the worst department in respect of functions but the best for studies in our college. It was the first event of our particular branch, and we were really excited about the function. It was mechanical's freshers 2k17 which has been finally finalized as we somehow convinced the teachers for the function.

It was decided that we are just going to a party and there will be no competition as this function is particularly for enjoyment and an introduction session of the first year to their teachers as well as seniors.

{Being used to physical labor as I am a sportsperson and also do each physical work like carrying cylinder to the kitchen at home I was already ready to be a mechanical engineer and also my particular love for bikes and real-world, and hatred for computers and virtual world I decided to pursue my B.tech in mechanical in spite of my parents' wishes to opt computers.

As the function was decided to be held on the 6th of November we have only 7 days to prepare when our seniors announced that few of us have to perform when teachers are present. I am a dancer but never performed alone cause in school I was mostly a loner and was determinedly focused on my basketball.

Before joining the college, I had made up my mind to participate in programs actively, so, I grabbed the opportunity and volunteered to perform as well as to help in decorations.

There was this senior named Sahil under whom all the preparations are going to be held. So, I approached him to ask how I can help, and he told me the necessary details about which I have to take care until the teachers are going to be present in the function. As the only girl who volunteered for the work, he gives me all the responsibility for the decoration.

I somehow managed to talk to my classmates whom I don't even know very well for help and all the ones those are my friends I already assigned them as my team. Sahil boss has this intuition that I can handle the decorations and he also had his theory that girls are always good at decorations.

I already prepared my dance performance on a Vandana as it's the first performance of the function. Now my focus was on decorations. On the 5th of November we took the day off for the preparations, Sahil boss was also present there with Nikita and Akash boss who is handling the scrutiny.

First, we made a list of the items we should be needed and then Sahil boss decided to go and purchase the required items. As I know all the items and was handling everything he took me along.

We were on the bike-sharing basic details of each other. As I am really friendly by nature, we became friends on the very first ride to the market.

The next day, we all were busy working and helping each other. I was giving instructions to basically everyone because by that time everyone was aware that I am working under Sahil boss, so they all have to listen to me, no matter they want to or not.

After a matter of time, we were ready with the decorations and all the preparations. Sahil boss was really impressed by my work and dedication.

And now it was time to welcome the teachers.

Chapter 7: Welcomed a New Member to Life

I have to get changed as it was almost time that teachers will be coming and I have to perform first. So, I ran to the changing room, get changed and came back in just 10 minutes.

When I got back teachers were already there and anchors were inviting the head of departments to ignite the lamp in front of Maa Saraswati as per the rituals.

After the ritual, I was invited for the performance, it was my first performance with the pinch of nervousness of performing alone. I performed well, at least according to my friends.

After the performance, I asked Sahil boss if my performance was good, but that time I didn't realize that his friends were standing there and that they can convert this friendship in a controversy. Also, as it was a Wednesday and I fast every Wednesday, I was not eating anything; Sahil boss noticed it, so he asked me about it and I told him about my fast.

He was also my kind as he told me that he too fast on every Tuesday. He said he has some sweet that can be eaten in fasts, so I followed him where he led me.

We actually went to the other side of the building, my friends were there already, and they were busy eating. Sahil boss got me the sweet but as I am the spicy kid, I insist him to eat some of them from my plate as that was too much for me. We ate in one plate and my friends did notice us.

This love of friendship was slowly growing between us by these small steps and I was not noticing the stares that were upon us. I was so much engrossed in our friendship and party that all I wanted was to enjoy with him. He became an important part of my life so fast that I myself didn't notice.

As much carefree I am I never worry what will the world around me say, I just do whatever I like. So, I danced and stayed with him almost all the time. That time I didn't know that my attraction towards him and our pure bond of friendship would get affected by stares around us and that my life is about to change a lot.

Chapter 8: Growing Bond with Hidden Feelings

So many memories established as well as so many pictures were clicked. The function was over but our friendship was growing stronger day by day. I told him everything about myself and vice-versa. As carefree as I was, he was the opposite, he cared too much about everything. As friendly as I were, he was an introvert and were generally remains in his inner circle. I was the only one that he got friendly with so easily.

In short, we were two really different people; our visions for life were also very different but still, we liked each other. We started talking frequently and soon our chats converted into frequent phone calls. I started giving him more time than I gave to my friends or boyfriend. He knows about my boyfriend, but he didn't judge me. Anyone other than him should have judged me about having a boyfriend and still chatting with some other person but he understands me so well that I never had to say anything.

The thing I like about him the most is that he was true, unlike others he never flirted but was always successful making me laugh. He was always helpful either it has to be in studies or in my life, he became my escort.

While we shared this great equation, we never let anyone know about this except for my boyfriend and Sahil boss's roommate because of Sahil boss's sake. He was my senior and very well aware of our college situations and thinking of students here. I simply respected his experience and never let anyone know. Of course, my friends had a hint, and they thought that I had a crush on him, that was true too but was hidden somewhere inside me. I never accepted that I had a crush on him. Hell, I didn't even know myself maybe because I like Prithvi a lot and he was my boyfriend, so I was never ready to accept. I never realized my own feelings.

One side I was not noticing the big mess that was coming but on the other, I was too much happy spending my days chatting and nights talking on the phone with Sahil boss. Soon our friendship got on another level when we met in a park in front of his room where he resides on rent. We were discussing past life and my life before college was not so great.

I tried but not a single word came out of my mouth, I just started crying.

"don't cry girl, otherwise your make up is going to get you in trouble ", he said. And I started laughing again.

"I don't wear any; you know except kohl."

"That's why am saying, you look bad ...crying and then you not even wear any makeup, so don't."

"I hate you."

"Haha, I know. Too much hate. UUffff! can't handle it."

Chapter 9: Hidden Feelings

Diwali was on its verge; college was off. Sahil boss and Prithvi were on vacation for the big festival. As Sahil boss and I were so connected and can't live without talking to each other we call each other every now then; somehow managed to give each other time in-spite of all the functions and rituals going around.

Sending each other pictures of our traditional wears and sweets and lightning was the best part we shared. After the holidays when we met, he brought me sweets in a small box as a token of Diwali. I was literally amused by his act.

We met that day only to exchange sweets, but then we get to know that both of us was free for the day, so we decided to go for an outing, I love traveling and who would have said "no" when you got an amazing company. But as big fool as I was and in addition to it I was quite lazy and I said no, the reason I gave was that there's a sun in the sky and I don't want to go in this weather.

So, we decided to go to his room and chill. We reached his room`, his roommate was not there thankfully. He was a gentleman as always, he cleared up his room before letting me in.

He was a senior but still, he didn't just prepare noodles but also served it as well as poured us cold drink in glasses. He didn't let me do anything. We ate from the same bowl and talked about everything. I presented him with a small gift after we ate. I bought him a smiley batch, chocolate, and a very small glass bottle which consists of a paper roll on which I have written "keep smiling" and then placed lots of small beads in it and fitted a cork at its mouth.

He loved the presents and we take pictures of them as well as of us together. We shared this great equation and have this strong chemical bond because he always knows his limits. We were alone in his room, two youngsters with intense heat and liking for each other but still maintaining the purity of the moment we were just looking deeply in eyes, never touched. Until my inner craziness and childish behavior get heavier on me.

We were talking about fitness as he was a perfect gym freak and we even talk on calls when he was on his way to the gym or back home. I told him to show me his and so he put up his sleeves and showed me his body. I don't know what struck me but what came out from my mouth was

"It's just good to show and say, if I will ask you to carry a girl now, u can't do that."

And then it struck me when he said: "stand up, and you will know."

I just got up without thinking and he really carried me but just for a minute and then it strikes me hard. That was the time when I realized that I got too far, I shouldn't have said that and shouldn't give him a sign.

He didn't take it the wrong way but I was not sure, I panicked thinking 'what he will think about me now'. I already have a boyfriend and still is going this far with him. I was a mess after this, I can't think straight. I didn't know what to do; I just decided to go with the flow and leave it for fate, but that was the biggest mistake of my life; I have to give a very big cost for neglecting my own feelings.

I wish I could have taken my decision myself instead of leaving it for fate, I wish I never had ignored my feelings; maybe things would have been different than. This age and hormonal changes and feelings that were developing inside me for two boys at a time got me in a lot of big mess than I thought, that I can never fix.

"कभी कभी कुछ किस्से

किस्से ही रह जाते है

दो दिल आँखों में ही बहुत कुछ कह जाते है

डर मै अपने

होठों पर जो ना आ पायी बात

कही खत्म न करदे

एक नयी कहानी की शुरुवात।"

Chapter 10: Realized That There Are Certain Things That Need To Keep Just With Yourself

I reached college to meet Prithvi the other day and told him everything about the last day that I was at Sahil boss's room and we talked a lot.

The look on his face changed suddenly listening to my confession maybe because he thought that something happened between us. But I assured him that nothing happened and that it was my own decision to go to his room and am comfortable with him. I trust Sahil boss a lot more than usual. I just praised Sahil boss too much about how gentleman he is and that he is trustworthy; that maybe Prithvi not liked him for that and trouble started coming for me from all sides from that day onward.

It's just me, Prithvi, Sahil boss, and his roommate Sanjay who knows that Sahil boss and I were together at his room the whole day.

Prithvi just listened to me and said nothing that day. I suspected his possessiveness and insecurity but said nothing as I expected him to believe me. I thought it was just a matter of time that he will also get to be friends with Sahil boss and then everything will be sorted out. We will all hang together. But life is never fair. It's a game-changer.

Soon I got to know what life had for me. Prithvi and Sahil boss already had some issues between them that I am unaware of. It was before I joined a college that they got into a fight with each other. This issue and their fight were over until I became a common link between them and blew the battle shell once again.

I have no idea what the hell was going on but one thing was clear that Prithvi doesn't like Sahil boss at all. He doesn't want me to get involved with him even as a friend, while on the other side Sahil boss has no problem with Prithvi, he knew everything and was ok with it. All he wanted from me was to be careful about my choices. He was clear about his thinking in front of me, he clearly stated that he will not comment or advise anything on my relationship with Prithvi. He just wanted me to be honest with myself and handle my things on my own.

A day after when I went to meet Prithvi he was in a bad mood. I had no clue about the thing going around. After asking more than 5 times he told me about the statements he heard in boys' hostels about me.

I heard nothing about any whisperings, but he said that there are many things that people are saying about me and my character. I also have friends in boys' hostel, if they had heard about anything, they definitely had told me. But that time my mind didn't respond. I just listened to him not thinking anything about the possibilities that this could be half a lie.

He told me that everyone knows about me being at Sahil boss's place for the whole day and that people are talking shit about me. They think that I am characterless and had an affair with him. Also, that I am cheating on Prithvi.

Actually, I am cheating on both.

Prithvi was very angry with me. He said he had a fight with some people too last night because they were saying shit about me, and he couldn't listen to a word. He also has to give answers to his friends about everything.

Like why, I was at Sahil boss's place? Why I didn't tell him beforehand? Even why I am a friend of him?

These questions were out of the blue. I couldn't understand anything. Maybe because this all was made up. It was our matter; I couldn't understand why his friends are asking him questions like this and why he had to answer? And what's a very big deal in it? When the matter is ours, he should have talked to me directly, why his friends? Friends stand up in the time of crisis not ask you questions like this to heat your mind up to some more.

I hate when random people involve in a matter of two and to be honest this reason for giving answers to his friends was shit but I didn't say anything, I don't know why?

Why he had to fight? He should have handled situations calmly. These questions were revolving in my head but I couldn't gather the courage to ask him.

These allegations on me and on my character made me go numb. I can't think of anything. All I was thinking was how anyone can know. I was too careful. I didn't tell anyone.

The only people know about this were me, Prithvi, Sahil boss, and Sanjay boss. Four of us knew about this. Why anyone of us will tell anyone about this when we know that if this thing goes out; this topic will become gossip and people will do our character assassinations. All of the three were my trusted people.

Sahil boss would have never told anyone; I trust him on this more than myself.

Sanjay boss is the most ever introvert person I have seen. He always remains in his own world or I can say in his limits. As I reached their place, he was already leaving giving us our privacy. Also, we trust him to keep this thing a secret. He will never betray his own friend.

I was told everything from Prithvi and when I told Sahil boss about this, he had no idea about anything.

But what's done was done. So, I decided to figure things out calmly by talking to both of them calmly.

I talked to both of them and tried to solve the matter out but it was too late. Prithvi had made his mind to kick out Sahil boss from my life, so he didn't agree on any of my points.

He wanted to meet Sahil boss and end this up.

That was the time when I realized that we shouldn't trust anyone on everything, people can use your confessions against you. There are certain things that you need to keep up only to yourself.

"जिस रिश्ते को हम सबसे ज्यादा मजबूत समझते थे

उसे ही बेसहारा कर दिया

बस एक ही पल मै

उन्होंने मुझे इतना पराया कर दिया |"

Chapter 11: Feelings for Both Got Me Stuck Between These Two

I was confused, couldn't understand what is going on and what role was mine. I tried to figure out every way possible. I talked to both, tried to solve the thing by myself. I don't want to involve anyone on this but Prithvi's friends start interfering which I didn't like. I am the kind of person who wants to solve her problems on her own and this ongoing battle was going out of my control which was unacceptable for me.

I was so mad for Prithvi that I was listening to his every argument, I wanted to say many things but can't say anything. I think people were right on what they say about attraction, you go blind when it comes to your feelings for your mate.

I didn't want to lose Sahil boss, so I accepted that all was my fault and I was the one who started to be friends with Sahil boss. But things were not in my favor.

The whole matter was revolving around me but I have no knowledge about anything. Boys were trying to solve it by themselves, and I was trying to solve it by myself. Things got worse because I couldn't get a clue what was going in their minds, I couldn't understand the situation. Many names started popping up in between, names I hadn't even heard before.

I was a mess, couldn't understand my own feelings. I tried to figure out myself first but couldn't. People were expecting me to be mature and stand for my own but I couldn't. I can't understand why suddenly I became a different person, lost my sportsman spirit, stopped eating, stopped chatting to friends, stopped visiting my family, most of the time remained quiet and still having always a smile on my face so that no one can suspect my ongoing battle with myself. I got stuck between these two, both were important for me; I wasn't ready to lose any one of them not knowing that I am going to lose both of them.

I tried to speak my heart out to Sahil boss but couldn't do that too, maybe I wanted him to understand my feelings without my words but that was not possible. He asked me so many times, tried to talk things out but all I was doing was crying, crying and crying. Maybe because my words weren't helping me, my tears were saying a lot.

The real thing was that my feelings were developing for both the persons at the same time. Different kinds of feelings for both but yes, feelings. And I didn't want to lose any one of them and this fear lost me everything. They both didn't realize this, but they got me stuck in between in their battle which was unfair, I have to go through all of this because they had a problem with one another.

These feelings were genuine for both, for Prithvi it was attraction and for Sahil boss it was affection. I tried to handle these emotions but I couldn't. I tried to tell this to Sahil boss but then this thought crosses my mind that this confession can produce distances between us, so I stepped back.

Stepping back cost me with a lot of things but made me stronger for the rest of my life My fears and not standing for myself was me back then, the old me but after this incident, I became stronger. I never step back now even if it will cost me bad, the only thing I gave up was my fears.

CHAPTER 12: Care for Me

Between all this chaos going on our college, the cultural fest was on its verge and preparations were going on full fledge. I was asked to perform a dance on this occasion. I was ready to perform, my solo performance on teacher's day filled me with the confidence of performing on stage, also it gave me a name in college because from that day onward seniors started approaching me themselves.

I was prepared for my performance. A singer was on road for the show consecutive was a "Kavi sammelan". My performance was the welcome performance for our guests.

I was in college the whole day preparing for the function. When I reached home to get myself dressed a new problem was waiting for me. I got to know that my father was ill, my mom didn't call me because she doesn't want me to panic. But she wants me to stay and don't go for the cultural night which was understandable but not acceptable. I tried to make her understand that I have a performance to give in next hour and how will they manage on this last-minute change with the welcoming performance but u know how Indian mothers are, once the order is given by her then I have to follow otherwise stay out of the house was the ultimatum.

I gave up in front of her as usual. I called the senior who was handling and helped him arranged the last-minute change. Thankfully my friend Deepika was ready to perform. She is a very good dancer and she has this wonderful thing about her that she is always ready with a performance. I managed the night but was full of guilt that seniors have to go through this because of me.

I was angry with myself and on my mom. She was right on her place, I didn't blame her but at least she would have told me before in the morning when I was leaving for college. I am 100% sure that I told her about my performance in the evening, but she didn't respond, so I left.

I am so emotional, I couldn't control myself and started crying. I locked myself in my room, didn't eat for the next 18 hours, neither get out of my room for a second. I also switched off my phone. All I was thinking was how I am going to face everyone now. I decided never to perform in college from that day.

My best friend Sashi called on my mom's phone to get to know about my where belonging but I refused to talk to anyone. I simply didn't respond to my brother who was standing outside my room with the phone call going on. My brother told Sashi about my anger and cut the call.

I messed up my room in my anger, break almost all the things made of glass. Get myself cut too with one of the broken pieces; slept crying.

The next day nearly about the evening I controlled myself; thought about the good times I have spent with my friends and family. I thought about how Sahil boss used to share his experiences with me and always protects me. His company, his talks always give me strength and a new perspective on life. One of his sayings struck my head, "never hurt yourself when life is taking your exam, it's actually a lesson that life is trying to teach you. So be a good student, learn the lesson and be ready to perform much better."

His saying gave me new dawn in that sobbing evening. I cleaned up the room, get some food and switched on the phone.

As soon as I switched on the phone, messages started popping on my screen. There were too many messages of missed calls on my phone from 5 different numbers out of which 2 were known. There were 4-5 missed calls from Sashi and more than 20 from Sahil boss. When I was checking true caller for the rest of the numbers Sahil boss called me. I picked up the phone and was relieved to listen to his voice. He has the same feeling on his side, but started his questions,

Where was I?

Why was my phone switched off?

Why I didn't perform last night?

Am I ok?

Etc.

I told him everything, and he scolded me for my childishness but then was relaxed knowing I was okay.

He told me how worried he was and solved the mystery of rest 3 numbers too, that was him. One number was his friends Sakshi, one was his roommate Sanjay boss and one was his 2nd number. There were more than 80 missed calls from these numbers, I realized how worried he was from these numbers of a missed call. I was sure that he hasn't slept the whole night and realized how mad I was that I didn't even call him last night.

He was such a caring person I got really mesmerized and amused when he told me about his meeting with the guests last night as he had contacts and how he arranged a meet for me too but that was my bad luck that I didn't show up. I still blamed him that he should have got an autograph. How silly I was! I know.

I didn't realize his care and love for me that day but now when I think of it, he was the only person who cared for me that much. Prithvi also knows about my performance and that I didn't show up but I didn't have a single missed call from him. But Sahil boss, he even asked my friends about me. That is why Sashi called on my mothers' phone to get my note on.

Sashi is an indifferent college but we have common friends.

The next day when I went college many people asked me about my where belongings and also asked me why Sahil boss was asking about me, that's how I know that he was asking about me. It's obvious, of course.

How dumb I was that I didn't realize that he was the only one present for me. I admired him, liked him but never showed or said anything maybe because I myself didn't realize his importance in my life until I lost him.

I still want to change that one decision of my life but obviously I can't, no one can rewrite past. I am just simply growing and living that feelings and memories in my heart till now.

Chapter 13: Biggest Loss of My Life

After the event life went back to the mess that was left to clear, finally they both decided to meet in my company not even asking me.

We chose the football ground for the meeting. Sahil boss was one of his friends while Prithvi was with his entire gang.

That day was the worst day of my life starting from a crack in my glasses, we were in class playing with paper balls to spend time when my glasses fell and someone put a foot on them, so, I have to bid a goodbye to them.

My spectacles have a large number and also it had been years since I use them. I am too used to them that I felt helpless as well as incomplete without them.

I and Prithvi went for the meeting together while Sahil boss was already there with one of his mates.

I was so devastated with all the college daily routine. It was already 5:00 p.m., along with that I was not ready to face both the men together. I was confused with my own feelings and emotions, wasn't sure about the meet. Actually, I wasn't ready to handle the happenings that would be following in or after this meet.

But time has going on at full speed and was not ready to listen to me.

Whether I want it to happen or not it was going to happen and I have to face it.

We bid wishes socially and sat down on the grass to start the chat.

Prithvi's friends sat a little further giving the three of us a bit of privacy.

The chat was actually allegations that Prithvi started on Sahil boss that he washed my mind against him that was totally wrong.

I was feeling like am a little kid of 5 who don't understand anything and these two bigger ones were taking my life decisions.

Prithvi basically started shouting at Sahil boss which I didn't like at all, I told him various times to talk to him properly, he is elder in age and should be respected.

Whatever we had to say we can say it in low voice with all due respect but I think he was not in that mood. Prithvi was full of so much rage inside himself against Sahil boss.

He was saying anything and everything to him but I said nothing, nothing at all.

Sahil boss tried to keep his side but Prithvi didn't even let him speak. Prithvi blamed Sahil boss for the happenings in the hostel, also, that he was responsible for the misunderstandings that our relationship was suffering, all the misunderstandings were nothing but about this mess. This issue was a big opportunity for Prithvi to kick out Sahil boss from my life and he grabbed it.

Sahil boss accepted all the charges while he did nothing. He showed Prithvi our messages in which it's clearly shown that I was the one who shared every single detail to him and I was the one who started being close to him but that also doesn't help.

At last Sahil boss just said, "I accept all the charges, its all my fault, but I am here for next 1 year as well as you guys, we will see if your relationship will grow or broke."

Remembering those moments, I can say that Sahil boss wanted me to say on his behalf actually to say for myself, to stand on my own. I lacked confidence that day because there was a battle going inside me. I wanted to take stand for myself for him but I didn't, I couldn't gather that much courage. I don't know what I was afraid of but I let him down.

He accepted all the charges to save me and to keep me safe because he doesn't want me to get hurt. He is just like that no matter if he is going through too much on his own; he will care for others first. After, all this drama we went our separate ways on terms that we will never get in touch again. That decision that they both took for me, it hit me hard but still I did nothing, said nothing.

I felt helpless, I tried to talk to Prithvi but he just shooed me away saying "go home", and I couldn't say anything after that. I just drove away. I watched Sahil boss walking away, it hurtled badly. I wanted to stop him make things right but I couldn't do anything, I just watched him going away. I should have done something but I just froze. I felt like am not myself anymore, felt so helpless.

The battle that was going inside me in addition to that the battle that was going outside, I lost both. Finally, that day I lost Sahil boss and I feel like I have lost a part of myself.

Sahil boss still was a gentleman for me, after everything he lost his image in college. He was the kind of person for whom the world matters, his image went down because of me in the 3rd year while I was in 1st year, from the last 2 years he has this Mr. Perfect title but I ruined it.

I was guilty, I am still guilty. The only regret of my life was this meeting. The only regret was that I didn't stand up, I didn't say anything, I didn't speak for myself, and I did nothing.

Now the thing is; what's done is done, I couldn't do anything now. I can't change time so no matter how guilty I feel, it matters nothing now.

I cried for the whole night that day for losing myself but that doesn't change anything, things remained the same. This loss is the biggest loss of my life, I couldn't lose anything more expensive than that now, not even my life is that much important because what I lost was not Sahil boss but myself. I lost my confidence in being me.

Sahil boss used to say "your past will never forget you even if you will forget it, past always play a vital role for your present and future, it will teach you how to handle situations in the future. So always value your past."

His sayings still give me directions in life and I am really thankful to him but also sorry for what I did and I will always be sorry.

Maybe he will forgive me but I can never forgive myself for what I did.

"दिल का हर पन्ना कोरा सा लगता है

तुझ बिन न जाने क्यों

सब कुछ अधूरा सा लगता है ।"

CHAPTER 14: Going through the Pain and Reviving

After all the mess life became normal again at least from the outside because it's just me who knows what's going inside me, how I was handling myself with all the loss and pain. I was broken, so much that I couldn't handle the pain and so even tried to kill myself taking sleeping pills but my family saved me, being a member of the family with medical backgrounds the thing stayed between the families and never revealed. I survived but the pain inside me was never-ending.

That pain was killing me daily. I even stopped crying. My tears that started remaining inside burned holes in my heart. There was too much burden inside me full of guilt. I couldn't forgive myself for what I did, neither had the courage to talk to Sahil boss again. Opposite of my nature, I accepted what life had for me. I didn't fight for my happiness or for my peace for the first time in life.

This loss made me too weak that I tried to kill myself, my parents never thought that a kid like me who already had seen too much in life and survived natural death twice can try suicide. I was always the liveliest kid in the family, everyone loved me for that. I was the most loveable kid in spite of the fact that I was the eldest, my liveliness for life inspires everyone; my family members always used to say that. This incident broke them too but being together we handled this phase of life too.

"दिल खून के आसूं रोता है, चेहरे पर फिर भी मुस्कान लिए फिरती हूँ

इस से ज्यादा कैसे बयां करू, की क्या हालत है मेरे ।"

Parents asked about the step but I told them nothing. They were worried about me a lot but I assured them this will never happen again. I felt their pain too when they were so broken having this fear of losing me. I lost someone but that doesn't mean that they should lose me, so I controlled myself and this urge of dying, I started living for them.

They know about me being such a good friends with Sahil boss, they have an idea that something did happen, but they didn't ask me when I said "it is my life, and I don't want you to take me back, I want to be strong and handle things on my own so please don't force me to tell you everything, don't make me weak."

My grandmother raised me because my parents are government employees. She is a tigress, a true spirit of boldness. She raised her 4 daughters alone, raised them to be good citizens. She raised them to be successful and now all her daughters are on good posts with supporting husbands. She raised me too, to be a survivor, to be strong, to face life alone and that's why she believes in me. She understands me more than my mother does; so, she helped me to fight with my own battles, asked nothing, just simply applied old methodologies.

I started spending most of the time with her and family. She used to tell me stories of lord KANHA that I had listened to from childhood but it was fun listening to them again. She told me all about her and my grandfather's childhood stories about how naughty kids they were and how they grew up next to each other, first being best of friends and then life partners.

She used to read Bhagavat Gita for me, cook my favorite food daily, started taking me to new places and also to the old ones where I have spent most of my childhood. This old methodology worked a lot. I started feeling better, the pain was subtracting, and the addition was happiness once again.

My confidence also started adding up again when she started taking me to gatherings which used to happen every Sunday near the only lake in the city in which people used to meet, contact and play different games as well as face competition friendly.

For my classmates, friends I was normal as always. I always keep the smile on my face as well as my chubby nature. Always disturbing friends between class and never being quite was me; if I remain quiet even for a while my friends easily suspect that something had happened. I don't want anyone to know about my pain, so I always keep my fun-loving nature of the above.

Slowly I revived myself and cried all the pain out and was back on normal but that regret was still with me.

I am really thankful to grandmother to help me out always and always being there for me if I survived this incident it is purely because of her.

If she was not there, it was possible that I had gone into a deep depression.

"कुछ देर थम जा तू ज़िन्दगी

कहीं छाले न पद जाये तेरे पैरो मै

इस क़दर भागते -भागते ।"

CHAPTER 15: Distanced Me from Prithvi

A month passed very rapidly, my contact with Prithvi became less after this incident. Sahil boss and I were not on talking terms, not even on eye contact terms. This incident distanced me not only from Sahil boss but from Prithvi too. He tried his best to know what's wrong with me, he tried to make me happy but none of it worked because I didn't want it to work. I was blaming every bit of it on myself and also some part of it on this relationship too not on Prithvi but on this relationship.

I still tried my best to keep up on this relationship but I couldn't. Every time I was around Prithvi I felt low and neglected, maybe, he didn't understand it but it was hurting me. All the happenings start revolving my head whenever I was with him.

After this incident, he started interfering in my life a lot more than ever, started making decisions for me.

I was a sportsperson and when I got the chance to play in college, he didn't let me go, I speak for myself that time but maybe he started thinking that I am his property or something, that day my heart cleared me up to give up on this relationship.

This relationship was hurting me and I could feel that but was not ready to give up on it because I don't like to give up on relationships ever. After everything that just happened I started feeling insecure about myself, I felt like I am like a bird who had spent her whole life flying but suddenly someone had put her in a cage. I felt suffocated.

My attraction towards couldn't understand that I needed time to process. He just thought that we need to spend more time together, so he planned on a trip with his mates. A trip that finally broke me and builds me to make the decision for myself. Prithvi vanished, I tried to talk to him, but he

CHAPTER 16: Break Up

The trip was planned according to him and I hadn't had any single clue about anything. I just simply followed him. I thought let's just give it one more try, and figure things out, maybe, this trip will clear things up but the trip made it worse.

Two days went well but after that Prithvi and his mates had a fight about something little that grew up into a bigger situation on the 4th day and Prithvi and his two mates decided to leave for our home town separately.

This incident seems to be weird for me, one side they were too united and on the other had a fight over such a little thing that they said they will solve inside their circle, then what happened.

On the trip, I remained as low as possible because I don't want to break up there when we were not in a safe place, not in our city. I tried to be a part of them so that I would not pick a fight there because I didn't want anything should happen there and go to any of the families of us.

Inside I was restless, always tried to ignore things, and was mostly on the call with friends or family. I had also spoked a few terrible lines to Prithvi because of my restlessness but somehow managed to control the situation as well as myself.

As decided, we traveled separately back to town. But after the trip, I spent most of the time with my friends to control the urge inside me of bursting everything out that my heart has burdened of.

Finally, one day Prithvi messaged me to meet him, maybe he had sensed my dilemma. I simply and calmly told him that I need to break up with him and without any questions, he just agreed on me neither trying to make amends nor asking about the reasons. Maybe he sensed my ingoing's, on the trip because I was so low on the whole trip, the fun-loving me was no more present there with him.

I was not feeling good to break his heart but I cannot show fake love to him. I can't regularly hurt myself to keep other people happy, so I decided on my own. Our break up made too many people unhappy but it gave me relaxation. After so much time I slept peacefully that day, when I was heading to bed I was feeling like I was going for a very long sleep that night, that I will not be going to wake sooner than years. That feeling was weird but peaceful.

CHAPTER 17: Being Single

Being a bachelor, I was happy again, no restrictions, no tensions, nothing and finally I could make my own decisions. I don't have to tell someone about my whereabouts of the whole day and all. No one was going to interfere in my life's situations from now on, I can take part in whichever game I want or whatever function I want. I can be friends with anyone I want without having anyone's consent. I can finally dance and no one will feel outdated about my classical moves. I was finally queen on my own.

I started living life like I didn't know anyone of them from this incident, like they were strangers to me from forever, of course, that was not true but I wanted my heart to be at peace, so I started working on myself.

I started hitting floors at night, taking classes at noon and hanging out with friends in my free time as well as reading books when I got time.

Books started becoming my new friends and I started spending hours reading. There were times when I just sit with a book at 10:00 p.m. and only get up when the book was done around 4:00 in the morning. Books became my new obsession and soon one year flawed just like snapping of fingers.

CHAPTER 18: Farewell; It's Time to Bid Goodbye

Time passed and it was time to end our 2nd year as well as to bid goodbye to our final year. It was a farewell. My sister gets me dressed as well as done my makeup. I wore a black dress and matched it with black heels, both of hers. She is my cousin just 6 months younger. Our sister's goals were perfect, we share everything including clothes and accessories. She is far much better in girls' outfits and makeup than me.

For me, people don't even consider me to be a girl from my outfit as well as the boldness I carry. I was always like this except that one time when I should be this bold and speak for myself and Sahil boss to save our pure relationship but now it doesn't matter how much I regret that. I don't know where my boldness vanished when I needed that.

Ok so my sister helped me to get ready, no other event took place whole year because of some government issues about the fund, and this was the first and last event of the year.

It was a black one-piece with pearls on it as design which I wore, she made a perfect bun of my hair and attached some beautiful pins to beautify it.

Also, she put on some kajal and mascara on my eyes and gloss on lips. I was looking incredible. But this was like a punishment to me, she kept me sit for more than an hour me being me was always as restless as the wind, cannot sit that much.

She did a very good job. When I reached the place every single friend of mine commented about how adorable I was looking. I was blushing to listen to those comments but people were like "you are looking like a girl for the first time in these two years".

It was a taunt as well as a comment but I liked it. People told me I looked like a doll and that was the most magnificent comment I got. My beauty was on a high level that day not only because of my looks but because I was happy from inside too. I was with my friends having a good time after the whole year. Events always have this positive energy that people forgot about their grief and start feeling positive or happy.

We have a ritual of giving respect to our seniors by welcoming them with a 'tika' and a sweet. It is the last day for seniors to enjoy and live to the fullest life of the college, so we tried to make the eve the responsibility of sweets. I was feeding them with sweets from my own hands. Gulabjamun was sweet and I was very well aware of how much Sahil boss was fond of it. He was there, of course, it was his farewell after all. It was heartbreaking that I have to finally say goodbye to him, that soon he will be gone, and that soon I will no more spot him in the corridors or in classrooms.

We were not on talking terms but at least I frequently spot him in college and was at peace seeing him good, healthy and fit at least from above because I know he will never be ok inside. What I did to him hurt him a lot. A lot more than I thought or can imagine. He never said anything but I knew him, I can understand him.

He ate the sweet from my hand all the way smiling. I tried to remain calm, was controlling every battle that was going inside me but that smile broke me. His friends took pictures but that doesn't hurt me but his smile; it made a deep impact, a deep hole inside me. I broke into tears. I just passed the sweets to someone standing nearby me and ran away direct to the ladies' room.

"उसने भी सितम को क्या हसीं बना दिया

मुस्कुरा कर एक निवाला यूँ खाया मेरे हाथ से

की मेरे अंदर दर्दों का समां जला दिया ।"

I cried my heart out. My batchmate saw me leaving the event, so he followed me, I tried to shoo him away from inside, but he just remained outside the door. I finally controlled myself and got out, he tried to calm me down, but I was so broken that my tears didn't stop. He asked me nothing but just gave me his handkerchief, made me understand that this was the last time that I can sort things out (he had a slight hint about the mess because he worked with Sahil boss and me on the first fresher's event) and took me back to the venue.

I couldn't focus on the program as my whole focus was on Sahil boss. I watched him throughout the event because I was aware of the fact that after this, I will never get to see him again.

I spent the whole evening seeing him enjoying, I felt happy that he was happy. I went home without eating because I didn't feel like eating, I just wanted to give one try, and maybe just maybe he will forgive me. So, I decided that I will meet him once to say sorry to ask him about his feelings for me.

"एक रात मुझे भी अपने मन की कर लेने दे

मुझे तेरी बाँहों मै खुदको भर लेने दे

तुझसे मुकम्मल करलु मैं अपने नशे का जाम

सिर्फ इस एक महफ़िल मै तू

मुझे अपनी जोगन बन लेने दे।"

 That night I couldn't sleep because I was waiting for the morning. I already knew how he is; he never forgives people that easily just like me maybe if he will forgive, he cannot forget and never be the same with anyone. I know this because I am the same.

"विदा कभी नहीं देना चाहती थी तुम्हे

पर ज़िन्दगी तो मेरे लिए रुकेगी नहीं

गलियारों मै ही दिख जाते थे

तो सुकून रहता था ठीक देखकर तुम्हे

अब छाले जाओगे पता है दिल को

पर फिर भी नज़रे ढूंढा करेंगी तुम्हे

की क्या पता किसी काम से कभी

यहाँ आना हो जाये

या उन्ही जगहों पर खड़े होकर

कुछ पुराने लम्हो की यादों में

तुमसे मुलाक़ातें हो जाये।"

CHAPTER 19: The Last Meet

The next morning, I called my batch mate Govind as he is in touch with Sahil boss from that first event till now. I know he can help me, so I asked him for help.

We called Sahil boss to ask him where he was and we get to know that he was at his residence. I knew his place so we went there.

When we reached, he was already awake and was just in a towel as he was going for the shower. Seeing me along with Govind he turned around and locked himself in his room. First, I thought he didn't want to talk to me but Govind told me about the boy's rule of clearing up the mess of the room before letting a girl in. He said he knew because he was the same and he was right, he opened the door after a few minutes and invited us inside, had a change of clothes and yes cleared the room. I requested Govind to stay outside as I wanted to talk to Sahil boss alone. His roommate Sanjay boss was smart enough to leave the room before I say anything.

I started formally because I didn't know where to start. I thought the whole night what to say and what to not but sitting in front of him I forgot everything. I couldn't even see in his eyes. I tried to say many things but said nothing except a few things.

I said sorry for everything and he forgave me too but his forgiveness was not enough for me because I couldn't forgive myself.

I asked him about how he feels for me, but he said he has no feelings now; he forgives me and also forgot everything but can't be the same to me as he was before.

I told him that I was afraid, I had battles and confusions inside myself, but he said if I couldn't say anything to him when he was so frank to me and never judged me then he couldn't help me, I have to say thing to him, I have to tell him, only then he will know. He was right on his side and I knew that but my words were not helping me. I couldn't describe my feelings, I couldn't say it what I want to say, I just wanted him to understand how I was fighting with myself. But yes, he couldn't read my mind I have to say but I decided to remain silent. I was always like that, I m so bad in describing my feelings but so well at controlling them.

I controlled myself but somehow, he saw the tears rolling inside my eyes. He doesn't want me to cry or I can say he can't see me cry, "Your make up will go wrong".

I controlled the tears too much, tried to look at him to make eye contact, but he didn't make any eye contact.

I said what was important to say "sorry for everything, I will be sorry for everything always, I can't fix the things right now but I wish I could forgive me if you can. The last day you just walk to me and eat that sweet with that smile on your face, that smile almost killed me. I felt that I saw you carrying dead me in your arms with not a single tear in your eye and that one moment that doesn't even exist killed me a million times because it felt like that dead me was actually the love that you lost. How can someone be so strong?"

He said nothing but I felt his silence that day. I bid him goodbye and left his place.

I was forgiven by him but not by myself but at least I had this satisfaction that I tried, that at least I said sorry when I had time otherwise maybe in future, I could regret this too. I knew that he would not talk to me like before, I knew that this will change nothing but I had this peace that I at least tried to say my heart out.

He always keeps his feelings to himself never tells anyone but I can sense what he was feeling. He was hurt too but showed nothing. I noticed the changes in him. He stopped managing events after the incidence as well as stopped a regular workout, maybe because the roads were no more his companions.

I remember how we used to talk over the phone when he was on his way to the gym. It was nearby, so he walks to it and we used to talk until he reaches.

That was the last time we met, had a talk. That meet gave me a bit of peace to my mind after the storm of last night.

That was the last time I had seen him. I don't know where he is now or how is he. He is married or not. I know nothing, years before Govind gave me a slight update of him, only that he is ok and was working with some MNC. I just wish him to be healthy, fit and successful always.

"तुम्हे पड़ना बहुत मुश्किल था मेरे लिए

चाहा तो था की दिल का हर राज खोल दूँ

हमारे बिच कड़ी अतीत की दीवार तोड़ दूँ

पर न अपने दिल को समझ पायी न तेरे

सब्द ही न फूटे मेरे मुँह से

पर आँखों के आसूं सारी कहानी बयां कर रहे थे

दिल में डर था

की जो खोल दिया मन तेरे सामने

तो मोहब्बत होने से रोक नहीं पाऊँगी

और जो मुझे हो गयी और तुम्हे नहीं

तो मै इतना टूट जाउंगी

की कभी जुड़ नहीं पाऊँगी

काश इस डर से मैंने थोड़ा लड़ा होता

तेरे मन मै झांक कर थोड़ा

थोड़ा अपने मन का कहा होता

जितना भरोषा किया था

उतना इकरार भी किया होता ।"

CHAPTER 20: Straight Forward

A few months had been passed as well as my birthday. I was now 20 years of age in July. August was starting with the start of a new semester for us. We had completed our 2 years of life span in college with two more to go. I changed a lot in these few months.

My point of view was changed towards life and relationships. But for me the change was good. I started living a very straight forward life. Yeah, it cost me a lot of things but it was for my own good. I was tired of being a good person always who always try to avoid fights; always try to save relationships. I finally started saying things straight on people's faces even if I have to lose that person, I was ok with that. Slowly I became alone but I realize that being alone was more peaceful than being around fake people.

When I started saying truths on people's faces, many old wounds started heeling. My heart that was burdened of too much complains, it started being empty. I lost almost every friend but realized that they were not truly my friend because if they were, they had listened to me and tried to solve this out but instead they choose to leave. While before when they had done something like that, I forgave them as well as behaved normally to them instead of leaving.

Being straight forward was a good change in me till now at least for me, my life started to be more sorted and peaceful after that.

I was in that phase of life when I didn't care if someone was even alive or not; people die daily, and they are also relatives to someone, this is life and we are here to be dead.

"If you think, you are right

Fine, you are right

If you think, I am wrong

Fine, I am wrong

Am not sorry at all

If you want to leave

No matter if you promised when the situations are okay

Just leave

If you want to stay

It's your choice

Don't force me to stay

If I am your priority, OK

Don't force me to make you my priority

If you feel for me

I respect your feelings

But don't expect me to feel the same for me

If you are at war with yourself

Don't disturb my inner peace

I am not interfering in your life

So, don't interfere in my life."

CHAPTER 21: Independence Day Got Us Together

It was August, 73rd Independence Day was about to come. Piyush boss was the coordinator of the function. It was his solemn responsibility to handle the function. Independence Day and republic day were the only two official programs that held very seriously in college every year.

I knew Piyush boss from the trip on which I went with Prithvi. He was also from Mechanical, so we became very good friends on that trip. I performed on each program from last two years but this year I didn't want to perform, I was in no mood to perform.

Piyush boss called me to say that some girls want to perform but they need help to improve their moves, so I went to the practice room where every participant was practicing. Piyush boss was leading some students who wanted to perform the drama while I had to lead 2 girls to improve their moves.

As this event was about the country as well as official important program, we have to report every single detail to our professors. They were also going to take a look at each performance before it should be performed on the stage.

Professors were always really strict about these programs and we didn't want anything wrong, so we did our best.

Piyush boss and I started spending whole days 10:00 a.m. to 5:00 p.m. preparing for the event and its performances. Each performer was the new bee; just joined the college from 1st august.

Spending the entirety of the day with them made us very good friends. They became so close to me. I started calling them "bacchas" as they were juniors, basically we started hanging out together. They have this positive spirit in them, a new selfless vibe; they just joined the college, so they had that new spark in eyes of a new phase that they are going to live. I was in 3rd year; had already seen too much, but they had no worries, no idea of what they are going to face soon.

The emotional traumas even between exams, friendships, breakups, attachments, fights, seniors, professors, and the loneliness were all a blur for them. Being with them I forgot about my own issues; I enjoyed their kid in them; they were like the old me when I was in their year.

The fun-loving and carefree nature while caring for other people's emotions was me once upon a time. Maturity with pinch of childishness as per situations. They were the same.

They were 18 in total; they became a family for each other as well as for me and Piyush boss. Piyush boss and I were good friends; we have worked together before, were comfortable with each other.

He was a final year still I didn't let him scold my kids even for a single time. Yes, they became kids for me and they too adopted me soon as their guardian.

I was never afraid of anyone, so I say whatever I feel directly to people, I did the same to Piyush boss; he didn't let him take the charge ever especially when he gets angry with kids.

Juniors started to think that we were dating because Piyush boss literally did everything I said. He also suffered a breakup, so he knew how it felt, of course, it was different pain but yes pain; this pain got us together. Spending time with him made me feel happy.

This family became my escort; I started being happy more than ever. My time was theirs now. We laughed, played, practiced, and shared crushes and feelings and much more. We shared our sorrows too. We named it "Nautanki family".

My bond with Piyush boss was a different kind of bond, juniors thought we had some kind of affair while we hadn't; they adopted him as their guardian too. Basically, we became a family of parents and 18 kids. Few of them were older than me but still, they became our kids and because of them we came closer.

Chapter 22: Confession

Step by step, day by day we climbed the ladder of bonding. From my day and his day, we started mentioning it as our day. We ourselves didn't realize how important we had become for each other, so much that whenever one was out of sight the other became restless.

At least I didn't realize that the peace I was searching for a while was started living in me. My restlessness was at ease, my days became happy, my soul once again was free-spirited, I started my childish behavior once again and he handled it so well. He handled all of it, even my anger and mood swings.

He was the only one on whom I started yelling and giving orders as I own him maybe because somewhere in my heart, I knew that he will come to me no matter what I did, he will just come back and make me laugh once again.

When he confessed his fondness towards me, I was confused. I didn't want any relationship because I had this thing in mind that I am not ready to handle another relationship. I didn't want to hurt myself again from my own mistakes. Because only I know if anything goes wrong again, I am gonna blame just myself for it not anyone else.

He just simply said, "I feel good spending time with you, my pain just vanishes. Please do me a favor, spend some more time with me even after this function."

I couldn't utter a word that time but I did realize that my feelings were the same; the pain inside me vanishes when I spend time with him, I did become restless when he was not around. I too wanted to spend more time but was confused because I didn't really want another relationship. I was not ready to suffer the same pain; my heart was not ready to suffer more even when I knew that it could work, that there is always a possibility. But I was too much hurt by my past that I was not letting go of that pain.

I was so stuck in that past that that pain became a habit for me. I was not ready to take the chance. I had this thought that what if we spend time together and he starts liking me for serious while I can't love anyone now for sure. I was so sure that love is not going to be a part of my life anymore; I was so sure that I am not going to love anyone now.

I just simply said what I felt instead of wiring it in words. This was one thing that I learned from the past; whatever the thing is even it leads to more confusion just say it clearly rather than leaving it otherwise it can lead to misunderstanding.

We talked it out and things became clear; even he was not ready for a relationship, but he just wanted to spend some time with me.

81

That gave me relief, I agreed on spending the time being together. We didn't know what to call this bond, what we really are? But all we knew was that we didn't give a fuck what will people think, we are happy together, enjoying each other's company and that's all that matters.

CHAPTER 23: Selection of Performances

Independence Day was just two days to go. As this was an official day all the senior professors, vice-chancellor and chairman of Indian engineering institute come to attend the program so our performances were first judged by 2 professors; if they approve then only we can perform on stage.

One of the professors was so strict, no students like him even no other professors like him. Strictness is ok, but he thinks himself to be the owner of the college, always act like this and say horrible things to anyone and everyone, no matter either it's a girl or boy or even a professor or student.

The biggest trouble in my life was that he was a professor of mechanical itself. I had to attend his classes in the 2nd year while in 3rd I opted for the other subject cause there was an elective option. He couldn't remember names, but he always remembers faces. I performed in functions for the last two years, so he knew me as a classical dancer.

Piyush boss also was his student and knew how he is; he was very selective in performances, never approved so easily. Dances had to be perfectly classical on classical music with no unrelated words or steps, drama had to be on the related theme with proper dress up and for the singing performances songs had to be in perfect raag.

We knew, so we already prepared the performances according to it but still, he disapproved of both the drama and the dance. Juniors got too upset and that's what Piyush boss was afraid of that if they got so upset, they will get demotivated and this is dangerous for their life.

I was not ready to give up so soon, so we tried again; he told us to change some steps in dance and approved it while he didn't even saw the whole performance, but he is just like that so being rude and he just wanted to maintain his "akad".

We are happy that at least our dance performance is happening. Our drama performance was disapproved of the reason that it was too religious while the theme was "Bharat chodo Andolan". The mime was all about how all religions got together with Gandhi Ji to fight for our nation, but he disapproved of it too, so we had no choice, we tried our best.

Juniors got too discouraged by this disapproval, I was unhappy too; they had practiced for it a lot even asked him before starting and he said: "go on". We were too angry with him but was bounded after all he is a professor.

I couldn't see my juniors too much upset and demotivated; their faces went dull, even Piyush boss gave up. This was not acceptable at all to me; I was not ready to give up so easily so just for motivating I start talking to them.

After, about 10 minutes talking regularly I managed to lit their faces up. They were so upset that they didn't even want to come for the function but it was our day of freedom, we can't disrespect our flag, I made them understand this. And at last we decided that we are going to perform, no matter if the professor approved or not; we will perform after the function is over, we will perform and make a video and will viral it. Listening to this they became a bit motivated and was back to happy faces.

They had done their best, so they deserved to be treated well, so we decided that after the function we are going to hold a meet and will decide for an outing and returned home to our blood family for the day.

Chapter 24: Independence Day

Independence Day was celebrated with rain. It was raining from the last 2 days and raining that day as well. The function was going too held in the hall than in the event garden. Rain couldn't stop us from celebrating the biggest day of Indian history.

We saluted our Indian flag with all due respect, gave our respects to our martyrs who gave their lives for us to be free.

My girls gave their best performance in white kurtas and blue jeans. We attended the function with all our hearts and almost forgot about the disapproval of the professor. We didn't perform any drama after the function but was still happy. We took too many pictures, even of the sweets that we got. We settled all the boxes together then took pictures, also took too many pictures with both boy's and girl's group along with the whole family.

After that we decided about the plan for an outing; we decided that we all will go for a movie as a family. Everything from bookings to vehicles was arranged as we were ready for our first family outing.

CHAPTER 25: Family Outing

The next day, we all met at a decided spot at the fixed time. We all were too happy to be together, when you got a family like this in college you are the luckiest person on earth. I was too happy to be with them; that was a different kind of feeling like it was my real family like I was with my own people, I love them too much.

We were 20 people together gone for our first outing as a family. We clicked a lot of pictures there too. We enjoyed the movie to the fullest, sat together, and ate together. As we are in a large number move for the cinema, so they decided to give us an offer on eatables. By that we realize how bonded we are that we didn't even care where we are when we are together, we enjoyed as we were.

Yes, enjoyment was fun but with that Piyush boss and I had the responsibility too of these 10 little kids as we were the seniors but juniors are all very smart, they took care that we both shouldn't have to worry about them. Unlike what I had seen in other groups that people went together but after reaching their destination, people separated into their own worlds; that thing was not in our group, they were always together, not leaving anyone behind. How could we even get separated as we were not a group, we were a family; chosen family but yeah family.

After this, our family became pretty inseparable. We started spending time together more than ever. Piyush boss and I also got closer day by day, the ice of confusion and insecurity started breaking. Feelings started showing themselves, holding each other's hand, hugging was our daily signs of showing fondness to each other.

We started preparing for bigger competitions to take our drama club on a new height, meetings started holding on a daily basis. Too many sorrows as well waves of laughter were shared, too much sarcasm and adulteries as well.

This family started growing when we met our kid's mates as well. We even helped some of them to get a girlfriend/boyfriend. We both were too cool acting like the coolest parents on earth to these 18 kids.

We started hanging out together, go on more outings refreshing memories that are going to last forever. Lots of drama along with these silly role-playing became our best of time.

CHAPTER 26: A Misunderstanding

As time passed, we got closer than ever before; didn't notice that we were now not that confused having each other and became more comfortable with each other.

Prithvi's best friend Priyansh boss messaged me one day to ask me something. We were good friends because of Prithvi; I knew his story of love too. He had a sad end too but when we talked once I assured him that one day when the time comes, he will be met someone; someone who will truly love him, someone he really deserves.

He messaged me about how my saying came true for him and that he finally met someone. I was really happy for him, as far as I knew he was a really sweet guy, so I was too happy that he finally got someone he truly deserves. He asked me to go on a trip with him as his girl will get some company; he didn't ask anyone else because he didn't want to tell anyone else. I agreed to go because I too was in a need of a break from the daily college routine.

I decided to take one of my friends with me on the trip, my friend Vijay and two of his friends had their girlfriends in Delhi whom I didn't know. But as per my extrovert nature, I blend easily with people so that was not my concern. Priyansh boss didn't want me to tell about his girlfriend to anyone, so I thought Piyush boss also didn't know about any of it while he knew. I didn't even give it a thought that he was in the same friend circle, so he may have known this.

This led to a misunderstanding. I told him that I was going with my friends that are not in our college but Priyansh boss told him that I was going with him. I didn't tell him because I had to keep my promise but Priyansh boss got me in this trouble.

We had a fight over it about how I didn't believe him to tell him the truth but it was not about believing it's just that I had to keep my promise. We both were right on our sides but this was the thing I didn't want; this is really why I didn't want a relationship. We didn't talk the whole night, but next morning we talked it out and decided to go together.

[The solution was too simple but humans are humans, we only made a big fuss out of it. sometimes life is just like that, solutions were present right under our nose, but we couldn't see it.]

We knew that we have to face many things to go together cause his friends didn't really know about us being together and as well as we knew them, we knew that they will make a big fuss out of it. Also, we weren't committed, we were just together without giving it a relationship status, so we knew that it's going to be so hard on us but on the other hand we also knew that we can face them.

CHAPTER 27: The First Night Together

Our first trip was the best trip I ever had because along with love, happiness, romance it also gave us some hard times and with all the ups and downs that we faced together, our bond became stronger.

We went for a four-day trip to Chandigarh. We wanted to take our kids as well, but they had their mid-term tests on the same dates and as we were not going on college permissions, we can't let them leave the tests.

We booked sleeper buses for us from our home town to Chandigarh. We knew that we can't tell Piyush's friend circle about us right now but somehow, they will know this, as after all Priyansh boss is also going, so we decided that we will handle this matter after our return. At that time, we just wanted to be together and enjoy our trip.

We didn't sleep the whole night on the bus except that I slept for two hours. We ate our dinner in our cabin only and talked about our childhood and families. Then the best time of our lives came, the attraction of youth, the fire of heated bodies, we got closer for real in that night of love. We melted in each other's arms while the cold breeze of air was touching us coming in from the windows and stars were shining like glitter dots on the black chart.

The night was full of shimmering love for me; like I am on a way to my like eternal destination. For me traveling in that night with him was freedom, a person like me who is not allowed to remain outside after 7 p.m. now gets to travel at night meant a lot. Even when I was not allowed to roam on my house's roof after 11, I was on a bus at midnight and was enjoying cold winds with empty roads and yes, him.

We looked deeply in eyes with a spark in them; our breaths mixed and lips met with their softness as well as loving emotions. Eyes were closed but our feelings were raising, we locked each other more tightly in those flowing feelings transferring the heat of bodies. Lip kisses went on and on along with neck kisses; we finally showed each other the attraction towards each other. The silence of love was in air and night went with that, the dawn of a new phase of our bond was rising. That was the first night I spend with him, that was our first night together.

CHAPTER 28: Night of Love

We reached the hotel that we had booked already online, checked in and got fresh. We all were hungry so went to eat something. While eating everyone except me was not ready to go anywhere, they were too tired by the journey. I was too tired but my being a traveling lover wants to visit more places as possible but the majority wins, and so we decided to go out in the evening while slept whole noon.

We slept the noon, twisting and turning in bed kissing each other half awake half asleep; enjoying our togetherness. Our first sleep-over together in that room having each other in arms under that sheet was the best sleepover yet with the best feelings of love. That day we truly felt like a couple. After getting up, I literally acted like a wife according to him. I selected his clothes for the eve and arranged the room properly.

We took shower one after another and got ready. We were going to a gurudwara, so I decided to wear a suit. I had a Punjabi suit that fits perfectly for the eve. It was a purple and green suit that I matched with white low heels, heavy golden earrings, matching bangles, black kohl, glossed lips and half tie washed hair.

He wore a navy-blue shirt with black pants and shoes. When I was getting ready he was staring me like he had seen me for the first time; I was really blushing looking at him staring me.

When we reached gurudwara we had to cover our heads to pay our respects, that's a ritual in the Sikh community. I had gone to many gurudwaras before but that place was too beautiful maybe I felt so blessed there because I had Piyush boss by my side and that was my biggest treasure. That love in his eyes when I covered my head with my chunni was the true love that every lover tries to find in their lover's eyes. That was the love and care that I really wanted, his eyes were saying a lot.

He said," you are killing me from your looks, you are looking beautiful my life. I love you so much."

That was the day when my love life complete. That night it rained a lot of maybe because it was too celebrating like my heart was.

For writers and people, sky cries but for me, it was the opposite. For me, it was celebrating and enjoying itself cause when it rains our mother earth grew, cultivated land got fertile, flora fauna, plants, forests all of our mother earth gets freshen up; it looks like a new life is born. Greenery starts blooming everywhere with fresh mesmerizing fragrance of soil in the air.

That night when we were leaving the gurudwara it rained heavily all of a sudden, while there were no signs of rain in the city. Maybe it was raining because I wanted it to rain, my heart is just like that whenever I was too happy, and I want nature to rain so that along with me this whole earth can become happy. As my mother says my concept of happiness was because of my name as it meant "mother earth".

We stand on an edge in gurudwara to protect ourselves from rain, I didn't want to get wet but was already too much filled with rain from inside "the rain of love". I was touched by how he stood in front of me so that no other random people can touch me as well as so that rain couldn't wet me. I just kept looking at him. I wanted to capture that moment forever with my eyes.

We waited till the rain gets slow and left the place as soon as we found the right moment. He didn't like south Indian food while I am so fond of it, so he said nothing and ate south Indian with me. He fed me with his own hands while I just sat ideal.

We were filled by so much love when we got back to our room. We were young, attractive and alone.

That night went with brief flames between two young people, Breaths were heavy, clothes were half wet, the light was dim, flames in the heart were raising and bodies were heated.

I looked deeply into his eyes, my feelings for him were on another level; he was laying on the bed when I pushed myself above him and forgot about the world. Our lips met again tasted like chocolate ice cream we just ate. We were ready to forget ourselves in that cold ice night while our bodies were heated.

From lips to the neck to every part of the body we tasted each other with pure love and affection. Under the sheets above each other twisting and turning we gave each other so many signs of that flammable night including love bites and nail scratches. That passionate lovemaking session went on and on through the night. Our first session of making love. It was nearly dawn when we slept cuddling each other.

CHAPTER 29: Too Much Shopping

Our morning started with a quick session of lovemaking followed by a shower together. That was always one of my fantasy to romance in a shower with my love that came true that day. Loving and touching each other under that water drops was like touching flames of fire with bare hands. Those moments were magical moments for us. The best part of our relationship was to show our love like that.

The rest of the day went on by visiting places, eating junkies and clicking pictures along with the group. But still, he touched my heart by small things that he did to take care of me. I always wanted someone to be so responsible for me. He used to walk always on the roadside, hold my hand whole time, took care if I needed something or not. Also, handled my childish behavior when I ran here and there; we also did a race that I won because he let me. I can take care of myself but these actions made me felt taken, made me felt loved, made me felt that I was really important to someone.

He was pampering me with all his love; that love made me happy, stronger than ever and yes, blessed.

The next two days we spent visiting some more places and then shopping. I did a lot of shopping there while I was the type of girl who didn't like shopping that much. I always went shopping with my mom or sister and never took so long to choose things, I was too quick with all of this because I don't like wasting my time roaming around instead I like traveling to good natural places or eating on stalls. I was like the one who went to shops when it was really needed otherwise I don't go.

But there it was different; I had the power to shop with my own choice with money in my hand. That was the first time that I spent hours shopping. The market was cheap there, so I shopped a lot more than ever. I purchased items of about 2000-3000 bucks while I felt like I had spent 8000-10000 bucks. The cause market in our town was not that cheaper. I even do the bargaining for the first time but was proud of myself to learn things that fast; even bargaining is a good thing to learn.

I purchased a leather bag for dad, lipstick for mom, a pair of sunglasses for my brother, a pair of earrings and a top for my sister. Also, I purchased some posters for my friends; and yeah, how can I forget my chosen family, so I purchased different kinds of pair of earrings for all our girls and keychains for all our boys.

For me, I took a topper, bangles, hairband, a jean, and too many earrings as the only accessory that I

was most fond of is earrings. I love heavy earrings.
I took almost 8 pieces of earrings for myself. Piyush
boss got mad handling my shopping bags, but I was
enjoying shopping for the first time in life. He
didn't purchase anything for himself, so I purchased
a t-shirt, a watch and a wallet for him. We also took
some items for his family as well which I selected
like bangles for her mom and aunt, earrings for her
sisters, etc.

Four days passed with these ups and downs; we had
faced some serious money issues too, but we
somehow managed it by lending some money from
friends. These four nights we slept cuddling each
other except for the first night but, now it was time
to get back home and spend nights alone once again
but we were happy spending this time together. Our
status was now officially together. That was the
start of our journey.

(We did this much of shopping but still when I got
home and hand over the gifts; they were like "you
should have done some more shopping if things are
so cheap, we would have given you the money for
that afterward."

This is how we Indians are, not satisfied ever but
that's human nature and it's good not to be satisfied
ever, once you are satisfied you will stop working
for your desires.)

CHAPTER 30: We Got a Problem

When we reached back to our home town we knew that we have to face his friend circle and that was what actually happened, the same as we thought it. We knew this was coming our way and that we had to face this one day, so we were ready for that.

His friends called for a meeting; I too wanted to go but Piyush as concerned as he is for me didn't take me with him. He wanted to solve the matter on his own while the matter was of us, so I was too upset with him.

He faced his friend circle alone but said nothing because he thought that it was all his fault that he kept this a secret from them but I didn't think that it was wrong. We both were not sure, we were just spending time together and if we kept it from them, there must be a reason; it was our life, our matter, they didn't have any right to interfere, but they did once again like they did when it was the case with Sahil boss, Prithvi and me.

I was too devastated facing the same again; so I decided this time I am not going to let this particular group interfere in my life. They had no right after all, but Piyush handled it all. He chose me over them so the discussion closed right there. I didn't cheat anyone, I broke up with Prithvi boss a year ago. He moved on in his life so did I, what was wrong in that. I was ready this time to face this bunch of people who call their circle "friends" while according to me they were not. Friends are never like those who always interfere with the cost of their own friend's relationship. They should have been happy for their friend, but they were instead of blaming him.

I too had friends and faced these types of situations too. Even a situation in which best friends dated same girl but at different time zones but it didn't affect their friendship. That was a kind of friendship that is true, not like these fake friendships.

The mainline that I always wanted to say to them but never got a moment to say was, "if your friend is keeping a secret from you than it's not necessary that he is wrong on his side, it is possible that there is some gap from your side. It's not necessary that always the secret keeper is wrong, look into your inner self too. Look about your behavior too, look if there are fewer efforts from your side, if your bond of friendship is not that strong."

But I know no person looks in himself, just blame others because it's not easy to accept our own faults but it's damn easy to blame others for our loss.

Chapter 31: Distance

Now that he had his choice, he was left alone. All he had left with was me and this "nautanki family". I had a fight with him for doing this but I couldn't remain upset with him for a long time and couldn't even leave him alone seeing the situations.

He tried his best to keep this thing from me but I could feel his loneliness, no matter if friends had issues between them, they can never hate each other. He felt lonely, no matter how hard he tried to hide this, and I sensed his feelings but had nothing that I could do in this matter. It was a pure waste of time and energy if I had tried to talk to his friend circle because I knew how their minds are.

He started spending his time among our kids and in classes but still when he got back to the hostel, I could sense his alone feeling from his voice. I couldn't see him like that so, I tried to spend my time with him. I too had a lot on my plate that time, a lot of work was pending due to the trip and I was suffering from a slight viral too. I tried my best but couldn't give him the time he needed.

Thanks to my luck, competitions were nearby, so he made himself busy in those preparations. At least juniors were there with him, so I was relaxed a bit.

That was a phase too; it passed somehow with all the ups-downs and high-lows.

Juniors performed well in their competitions, secured positions in a few and were preparing regularly for the next ones. The family grew together.

Piyush and my bond got much bounded by all the love we showered on each other with unexpected surprises, monthly anniversary dates, unnecessary fights, long fun meetings of the whole family, family outings, long late-night talks, loveable trips and some pain of distance while exams and general holidays.

Our whole year passed with this hoe. Our family became the perfect example of a friend circle in the college. It was about time to bid farewell to Piyush boss while I had one more to go. The whole year with too much love from him I was not ready to let him go but I had to. This time the distance between us is not going to be for just a few days but maybe years.

That feeling of biding goodbye was hurting badly, not only to us but to our juniors as well. A part of our family is leaving after all. He was not leaving the family or the world just the college but still, we were so hurt. I literary cried the day he left, but he made me laugh that day too. With tears in eyes and smile on lips, I bid him "bye" not a "goodbye" because I knew he will come back to me.

The next year I spent on my own. With him, in college, I can call him anytime to come and meet me but afterward, I didn't have that privilege. So, I just simply minded my own work, attended classes and got back home most of the days.

Some days I spent with my family but my mind wasn't present their fully cause my half part was not there, I always missed him. We talked to him on video calls when we were together and sent him photos of the outings; we really enjoyed our outings but for me, his absence was always there.

That year I spent just with my chosen family, and my work in college; this became my world for me. He was doing MTech while I was trying my hand in writing. We talked on calls and met in months or so but those meetings were full of love. That distance made us realize how important we are to each other; how incomplete we feel without one another.

Year passed by and I finally graduated from the college with a placement in hand. We had to spend two more years apart until he is done with his

MTech along with a secured job so that he could talk to his family as well as mine.

We were not afraid of the fact that our families will not support because we are from the same cast as well as our families are okay with love marriages.

Two years of time too passed; apart from distance but close from hearts, our love was always bound by strings that connect us together. These two years were full of Surprise visits, long calls, video chats, distance-aches, misunderstandings, small fights, and patch-ups.

But after all these highs and lows our family stood together. We were still in touch with everyone on conference calls and video chats; once Piyush and I even visited college together to give our kids a little surprise for a sudden and once again went on a family outing like old times. That was the final year of our kids "humare bacche bade ho gye hai", they had become seniors after all.

We talked a lot, relived our memories, spent quality time together and had a lot of fun. We had passed an amazing phase of life.

CHAPTER 32: Introduction (Girls)

I already had talked a lot about my kids, maybe it's time for me to introduce them all to you guys. Let's start with my sweet little innocent girls.

Our girl's gang had every type of girl really different from one another, unique in their own style but still good friends to each other.

Sikha: She is a grain of wheat with glitter eyes. She always has this smile on her face that even lit up other dull faces. An extrovert with good health, height, and weight; with a heavy sweet voice and excellent dance moves. A good learner, the powerhouse of the family. Also, the Ludo lover like me. We had played Ludo a lot at our times.

Meesha: The quiet one. She was the quietest one among us; only speak when necessary. The slack one with fair color and beautiful body poster. She is the bomb in the group, either she is just quiet but when she comments or says something, it was like a bomb of sarcasm.

Bhumi: She with dark color has an amazing body posture. Her features are sharp and Indian that's why she looks so gorgeous and sexy both at the same time in an Indian traditional dress. She is the most "shaitan ladki" but most sensitive one.

Kanika: She is the same as Bhumi "shaitan ladki", so they have this great bonding with each other that sometimes people think that they are having an affair. Kanika is thin with ok height and loving nature. She always took my side whenever I and Piyush had loving fights. She loves me more than anyone else so Piyush was like "miss boss ki gaud mai jake beth jao, jab dekho tab miss boss-miss boss krti rehti hai".

Tanushree: Tanushree was thin but cute. Her nature is amazing, she is quiet at times but observes everyone. She is the one with the uttermost patient in our gang. She lives in her own world but values relationships a lot. I love her hoe.

Deepika: She is the "chulbuli" one in us. Always ready for some fun and masti. With fair color and good height, she looks amazing in her looks and is really good at making friends easily.

Harshi: She is the one with a great personality, she carries herself so well according to the situations. At serious meet times, she always remains serious otherwise while having fun she was fun-loving.

CHAPTER 33: Introduction (Boys)

Our boys too are different from each other but all are lovely as well as "harami".

Priyanshu: he was my junior in school as well, so he calls me "di" instead of miss boss. He is a guitarist with fair color, good height, loving nature, and a loud pitch voice. He is Piyush's advisor as well as a secret keeper when it comes to surprise me.

Prakhar: He is too included in the group of Piyush's own gang, they always plan surprises for me together. Prakhar was the one to arrange the things for the surprise they had planned. He is tall and healthy with fair color and an awesome sense of sarcasm. He is very well aware of Piyush's weakness; so, he always took my side and we both make fun of Piyush a lot.

Rohit: The "shaitan" one with always fun in his mind. He is the one who irritates all but is the powerhouse of the family. Everyone remains happy around him as well as fights with him. He is the cheater one in Ludo. He has a wheat color with slightly curl small hair.

Gaurang: The "odd one out" in the gang. He always focuses on a topic when we all were over discussing the topic, but fair with handsome looks makes him attractive that's why he dated an MBA girl when he was in 1st year of B.tech. "Launda sahi khel gya."

Sumit: Always the quiet one who always remains a step back from everyone. No one really listens to him but when he became angry his face becomes red and everyone did listen to him.

Mohit: The money lender. With a healthy body and wheat color. A fun-loving guy with a good sense of sarcasm timing.

Manas: The quietest but observant person who remains in his own world but is very well aware of happenings around him. He is slack but with fair color and good height. He does very good acting like a drunk.

Shivang: He is the best of all in acting like a drunk person, even when he is not a chain drinker, it looks like he is. He just carries his water bottle all along and regularly drinks water from it like he is drinking beer or something and then act like a drunk; even from his eyes, it looks like he's drunk.

Sandeep: He always remains in his own world only. Always has his phone in his hands if we are not practicing. He remains in his limits and only speaks when needed.

Harsh: The lover boy with his innocent looks and cute face.

These were my boys, but they were not so innocent, all are really smart that they can outsmart anyone but still I love everyone; all my girls and boys.

CHAPTER 34: Dates Are Fixed

After all this time we couldn't stay apart anymore, so we decided to talk to our families for the big decision of our lives.

I told my grandmother first because she deserves to know after all she raised me up. He met Piyush even before telling my parents and she liked him a lot.

Piyush was nervous before but I just simply advised him to don't act to be nice because he is already nice, my grandmother liked him because he showed what he was as I advised him. His nature and love towards me were visible so my grandmother approved him in the first meet itself.

She talked to my parents for me and there, Piyush talked to his parents; our parents decided to meet each other for our sake. When they met we were too nervous and afraid and they were too, we didn't even know what is going to happen but we were positive. When they met first they were little, my father asked various questions to Piyush which he answered half confident half nervous, same as me as I answered his mother's and sister's questions.

After all the questions and answers they were satisfied that we are a good choice for each other, they were not sure but because of our love, they said yes to us.

That was the first time when Piyush and I met each other's families. We were ready to live together, but I was too afraid because I have to be the one to leave my house and live with him as well as his family.

I was afraid about the responsibilities that will come upon me, I was afraid if I can handle the home, if I can blend it in better family or not; my heart was asking me so many questions that I couldn't answer but one thing I was sure of was that no matter what, Piyush is going to be at my side always; that no matter if I will mess things up he will protect me, will help me in being a good wife as well as good daughter-in-law.

Dates were decided, preparations were started. It was the month of October when dates were decided which was 14th February. We didn't decide it, the Pandit Ji did; maybe it was already destined, so we were getting married on Valentine's Day itself.

 As far as I love the Hindu rituals of marriage, I love the rituals of Christian weddings too, so I requested Piyush that we will do marriage as per Christian's rituals too. Piyush was okay with that, I knew Piyush will do everything for my happiness but it was difficult to take permission for this from our parents. It was hard but somehow, we managed to take their approval.

The destination for our Indian wedding was Jodhpur while for Christian rituals were Goa. Only 3 months were left. We were so excited as well as nervous.

For me, it's the last 3 months in my own home with my own family with whom I was living for the last 24 years, who raised me, made me a good person. For me, it's a mixture of feelings. On one side I was leaving everything behind like whatever life I have lived before was nothing, everything is going to be a blur for me while on the other my new life was awaiting me opening its arms wide with a new family, new love, and new responsibilities.

That three months passed like a wind of gust. My whole family was too excited about the event, parents were busy making the arrangements from my clothes to the clothes of my to-be family.

I designed the wedding card on my own. It was a beautiful small peacock that was embedded with beautiful colorful stones that will give a voice message invitation as soon as they will open its wings. All the peacocks were distributed.

Those relatives to whom we hadn't even had any contact for years are also invited after all I am the only daughter to my father and it's a dream for every father of a daughter to make this big day the best day for his daughter. My father is doing the same, he didn't want a single misshapen at my wedding. Everything should have to be perfect and he made it perfect.

"वो जताता नहीं तो क्या
सबसे ज्यादा प्यार से भरा वो ही होता है
दर्द क्या होता है उस पिता से पूछो
जो नाजो में अपनी बच्ची को पालकर
कन्यादान कर देता है।"

CHAPTER 35: The Rituals before the Big Day

It was the 7th of February, the rose day on which the rituals got started. Our close friends and families were already reached a night before, my kids too.

On the night of 6th Feb. Piyush arranged the most beautiful surprise for me. On the terrace of the event venue that is "rattan palace" in Jodhpur, he arranged a date for us. It was so beautiful, I didn't expect anything on this night, after all, we are getting married, that is enough function especially when you are the bride; as people say the wedding day is the bride's day.

The terrace was decorated with rose petals and fragrance candles. There was a table in the middle with a bottle of champagne and glasses. Red helium balloons were also attached to the corners of the terrace. He once again proposed me for marriage sitting down on his knees with a beautiful red rose. It touched my heart, I was on the seventh cloud, my happiness had no boundaries; I couldn't stop my tears nor my smile. I am lucky that he is my husband in the near future. He loves me a lot; this action proved that no matter if we are getting married the bond between us will remain the same, the love will remain the same, and the surprises will remain the same too.

It's the best feeling ever, I felt so blessed having him in my life. We shared our feelings that night about how nervous as well as excited we are. This mixture of feelings was giving us goosebumps, but we promised each other to be there for us, to face the ups and downs together, we believe in us that if we are together, we can face it.

"हाँ, छूते हो तुम मुझे

जब आखों में आखिरी ख़याल तुम हो

खुशनुमा है पुरा दिन

जो दिन की पहली शुरूआत तुम हो

भुल जाती हूँ मुझपे लगे जख्मों के हर निशान

जब मेरे साथ तुम हो

एक अलग ही दर्द-सा उठता है सीने में

जब मेरे पास तुम हो

हाँ नहीं है भरोसा तुम पर

इस दुनिया की भीड़ का हिस्सा तुम हो

फिर कहीं से आवाज आई एक दफा कर तो सही यकीन

शायद भगवान का भेजा कोई फरिश्ता तुम हो

हाँ ढलते सूरज में चांद देखा मैंने

जैसे उगते हुए चांद मे दिखे सूरज तुम हो

बहते हुए पानी ठंडी हवा के बीच

मेरे पास बैठी शांति तुम हो

मेरे हाथों में खिलते गुलाब की

महकती खुशबू तुम हो

खिड़की से आंख में चोली खेलती मुझे गुदगुदाती

सूरज की वो किरणें तुम हो

निहारती हूँ रोज जिसे

परिंदों का वो घोंसला तुम हो

पूरी करूँ अपनी हर ख्वाईश

की मेरा हौसला तुम हो

जज्बातों को बयान करूँ जिनमें

वो अल्फाज तुम हो

मेरी रुह गुनगुनाती जिसे

वो आवाज तुम हो

सजदे में मेरी प्राथनाओं कि

आस्था तुम हो

जैसे मुझपे माँ का लगाया

काला टीका तुम हो

कहीं गुमसुम हो

शायद मेरे ही ख्यालों में खोएं तुम हो

शायद सामने हूँ तुम्हारे

पर मेरे ही इंतजार में पलकें बिछाए बैठे तुम हो

शायद मुझसे ही कामिल तुम हो

शायद मुझमें ही शामिल तुम हो

हाँ मेरी पहचान तुम हो

मेरे होठों पे चहकती मुस्कान तुम हो

मैं पूरी मैं नहीं

मेरा आधा हिस्सा तुम हो।"

The next morning, Devi Sthapana pooja was held for which we dressed up in white. We already matched our clothes for the whole wedding. It was all decided, not only for us: the bride and groom but the whole family.

The hall was decorated with beautiful white flowers and a white-blue combination of balloons. I wore a simple white lehenga with golden chunri and matching accessories. Piyush wore a white kurta-pajama with Rajasthani jutiya.

Pooja was important as per the rituals but it was so boring as usual. Thank god, after 2 hours it got over with no worries.

The next two days were assigned as the last days of being a bachelor so these two days are for fun for both of us. We arranged a bachelor's party for our families too, not like that but in a decent manner. For all the men's a poker game party in the night and pool party at noon. For the ladies, mocktails party at night and kitty party at noon.

For us, it's the real bachelor's party; as much as I listened from my kids, they enjoyed a lot. I was okay with all the arrangements, it doesn't matter if girls were there as waitresses at the party, I believe my man.

They enjoyed their night dancing and partying a lot and on the other hand, our hen's party was on full volume too. The only day I was waiting since forever was this "the official hen's party". I wore a red bikini as I always wanted to wear, open hair and red high heels added charm to my beauty. I entered the venue as a queen; I was after all for that night. With my 5''8 height, wheat grain color, smoky eyes, glossy lips, heavy metallic earrings, and perfect figure I looked so sexy in that bikini. I especially had worked out for the last three months for this day. It was a rain theme party along with all the mocktails and cocktails which were served by half-naked men.

All my girlfriends looked so sexy in their bikinis, we enjoyed the most with every shot of vodka and danced the whole night. We were too tired the other day that we slept the whole day -night.

On the 10th of Feb., it was our engagement day. As I wanted, it was in the garden rather than in a hall. Most of my family and his family had arrived by now.

It was evening, I got dressed in a beautiful light blue lehenga as I wanted, off-shoulder blouse, royal blue net dupatta, heavy earrings, blue bangles, blue heels, glossy payal, designer bindi, Kamar bandh, and bajubandh too; as we were in Jodhpur I wore each ornament according to the Rajasthani culture including the maang-tika. Blue is my favorite color after black, so I selected this blue color lehenga for our engagement; for him, I selected a royal blue sherwani with golden dupatta and white pajamas.

We exchanged our rings in front of everyone at the perfect timing of stars. We were too happy as we had stepped one more step forward in our relationship. The following was dinner and refreshments for the night.

At night, we had a beautiful photoshoot; clicked too many pictures in different postures for the wedding album. It was so romantic; I am at a lack of words.

"जहान भर की खुशियाँ मेरी झोली में भर गयी हो जैसे

सितारों ने मेरा आँचल सजा दिया हो जैसे
ऐसे चमक उठी है ये रात सुहानी
खुदा ने खुद अपनी इनायत बरसाई हो जैसे "

"तुम्हारा औरा मुझे तुम तक खींच लाता है

तुझपे फना होने को मेरा मन मचल जाता है
मैं आँखों से पी लेती हूँ तेरे बदन के छलकते जाम
खुदको मैं तुझमे समां दू ये मेरा जी चाहता है "

The next day we had the ritual of "haldi". This ritual is done so that on the day of the wedding the bride and groom should have a glow on their faces. Haldi has turmeric properties.

From this day I and Piyush are not allowed to meet so far to the time when there was a net between us when we sat on the 'Patta' for the ritual. 'Haldi' was a fun ritual to celebrate along with its beauty of simple clothes and accessories.

 I wore a saree of a single cloth of yellow color with accessories made of fresh flowers. I was looking like a princess of history. Piyush wore just a white dhoti and he looked so hot in that. First, everyone applied haldi with their blessings to Piyush; after which the same haldi was were to me. My girls and family applied haldi all over my body, so I did the same I too applied haldi to them; it was like we were celebrating Holi with haldi. All the family too started acting like us and we literally celebrated Holi with haldi, applied it to everyone's face and hands.

We had to go for the bath as we all were covered in haldi so what I did was childish but enjoyable. As the ritual was in the garden, there was a pipe at one corner connected to a tap, I turned the tap and just showered the water on everyone, it was too much fun. My mom scolded me a little for my childish behaviors but cooled down soon because she too enjoyed it. It was looking like marigold flowers are dancing in the rain as we all were too much yellow because of the haldi as well as our dresses that we matched to be yellow for the day.

The next morning, we get up fresh and got ready for the Mehendi ceremony. It's my Mehendi, as much as I was going closer to my new family, I was feeling sad and broken with the feeling that soon I am going to leave my family behind for forever.

A woman is always a daughter but not like before when she became a wife too. Her family changes and that is a really huge change. Even if your husband is too supportive, even if he keeps your family as his family but your parents will never treat you like they used to be before marriage. For them now you are someone else's family member, you will just be a guest for them.

We wore green for the day, Mehendi walis were invited for the event so that they will make beautiful Mehendi designs on our hands. As I am the bride, the ceremony started from my hand. I had to sit for 3 hours for the Mehendi to be done, it was just exhausted by just sitting still for that much of time while everyone got free early and were dancing.

Today even Piyush had to apply Mehendi as he is the groom, I loved this fact that close family men's too had to apply Mehendi because now we were on the same page.

My Mehendi was too beautiful of both hands and legs, as I am the bride my Mehendi was the longest, it's till my elbows. It took too much time to get dry but at night when I washed it, its color got so beautiful and dark. As per sayings, the darker the color of mehndi will get in your hand the more love you will get from your husband.

Piyush Mehendi was also dark and beautiful. He couldn't find his name firstly in my Mehendi but after a few minutes, he finally found it.

That night I slept with mom because of the feelings that were making me cry. I couldn't help but think of life without my parents, I was sad that I am going far soon, that it's just 2 more days left.

CHAPTER 36: Best Wedding Ever

Its 13th of Feb, it is my wedding day tomorrow. Today is the sangeet ceremony, everyone includes me and Piyush rehearsed for our particular dance performances the whole day.

In the evening, stage and place were decorated with hanging candles, Rajasthani folk dancers were invited, and everything was decorated as per the Rajasthani theme. We all get dressed up in Rajasthani dresses. Rajasthani dishes was prepared, dress code was jodhpuri kurtas for men and jodhpuri lehengas for women.

The night was full of fun, everyone danced a new dance form of their own. Basically, only the expert dancers showed us the real Rajasthani folk dance, others tried but couldn't succeed but everyone performed well. We enjoyed the night; my mom's dad, as well as his too, danced on old Bollywood songs. My boys and girls danced on different Bollywood songs representing our love story.

They acted us too good after all they all were actors, they represented the journey too well, there were some moments when we really got embarrassed because they were some private moments no one knew about but the whole act was mesmerizing and worth seeing.

And finally, the day arrives. The day I was waiting for, the day for which we have been preparing from the last few months, the day which has been our dream. The day when finally, "and you will become us".

Everyone is here in Jodhpur for our grand destination wedding. My family, his family, all the relatives, and friends and of course our sweet little but not so little 18 kids.

All my 8 sweet little girls are helping me to get ready for this big day and so here I am sitting in front of the mirror savoring my last few minutes of being a bachelor. I am on the seventh cloud and looking at myself thinking about all the good and bad times that we suffered to finally reach this day.

Yipeeeeeeeeeee………..finally the day has arrived and I can't believe, but I am the bride; yes, I am the bride. My all little girls are looking beautiful and now they are happily welcoming their dear pops who is on the 'ghodi'. And of course, as per rituals I am not allowed to see the 'baraat'. But I know how happy everyone is and how madly my 10 little boys are dancing in the 'baraat' after all we have the technology, at least I can see my 'bacchas' if not my husband to be.

Now it is my turn to go-ahead to the stage. My heart is pounding so fast. "Kahi mai Khushi ke mare marr na jaun".

Looking like a doll in my red and golden lehenga with "jari work" and net dupatta, I am walking towards the stage. My heavy gold set with matching earrings, red bangles, and red heels are glittery and this new look with good makeup is giving me the touch of beauty. I am walking on this path of red roses having a red chunar above my head as per the rituals. The path got fully covered with rose petals because Piyush doesn't want me to step a single foot on the bare road on this big day of our lives. Everyone is looking at me to judge me on my looks but Piyush is looking at me out of love. And all I care about at this very moment is him.

How amazing is life can be I wonder, we had been preparing for this day for months, I and Piyush had been dreaming this day for years and now its finally here.

Piyush is looking extra handsome in his golden sherwani. Seeing him I am like, "oh my god, this man is mine."

"My stomach is full of butterflies."

The hall is decorated with orchids, candles, balloons and the stage is decorated with white peacock statues and feathers.

It's a big hall and now everyone is enjoying dishes, we arranged for every type of food from Rajasthani to south Indian to Kashmiri to continental.

After, all the photographs and garland ceremony we are nowhere in the "mandap".

I wanted the garland ceremony to be simple because I don't believe in showing up, the rituals are not for show. The other ceremonies happened between the closed ones, so I added themes and pinch of salt to them but not for this one ceremony.

Now it's the time for the most awaited rituals, the pheras,

We are finally tied into a knot, with every phera we promised the 7 promises of marriage with all our love. Revolving around the fire I felt so different, so blessed, with every step I prayed for a happy life ahead, with each step I made a promise to myself to try my best to keep Piyush and his family happy. I prayed for my family too, I prayed that I will get the strength to support them too.

 When he finally tied the "mangalsutra" around my neck, I have goosebumps; "sindoor" the last but most important sign of the marriage is done with all the mixed feelings. I feel so blessed, I closed my eyes to feel the whole moment. This was the biggest moment of my life, that feeling that I am a wife now was marvelous, can't explain in words.

"इस रात की चका-चौंद में

मैं तेरी बनने चली हूँ
सजकर लाल जोड़े में
मैं तेरी दुल्हन बनी हूँ
थाम ले मेरा हाथ
और करदे मुझे मुक्कमल
भर दे मेरी मांग
और कह दे इस दुनिया से
अब में तेरी अर्धांग्नी हूँ । "

This night is the best night of my life; this wedding is the "best wedding ever."

Tomorrow, I and Piyush will take a flight to Europe. Our marriage according to Christian rituals is going too held there, as our parents are not that modern to approve us to have this marriage among our relatives; we decided that we are going to do this alone, just the two of us.

END

It was hard for me to leave my parent's house, we are here in Jodhpur not even in my home town but as per the rituals I have to leave them behind, doing that ritual I felt so bad, so hurt that I couldn't stop my tears.

My parents cried too and that was the worst part. I am going to miss everyone. I am going to miss our family gatherings, our small unending fights, my grandmother's food, basically just everything. I am going to miss my whole childhood.

But the new life that is welcoming me is going to be better, I have an intuition. So along with all the hopes and happiness and sadness, I am going to sleep because I have a flight to Europe in a few hours for my Christian marriage and honeymoon.

That's all for tonight. See ya guys.

THE END